This book belongs to

_____

WALT DISNEY®

CHOOSE YOUR OWN ADVENTURE®

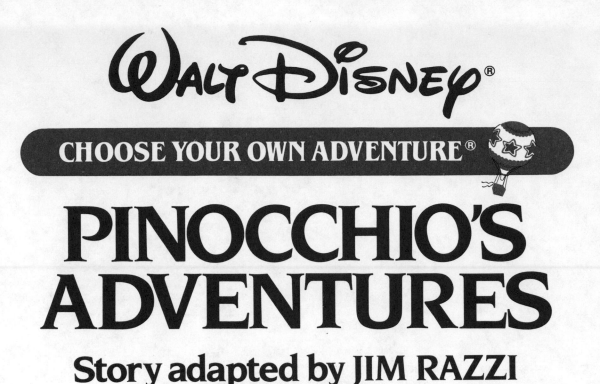

PINOCCHIO'S ADVENTURES

Story adapted by JIM RAZZI

Bantam Books

TORONTO · NEW YORK · LONDON · SYDNEY · AUCKLAND

RL 2, 004–008

PINOCCHIO'S ADVENTURES
A Bantam Book / March 1985

CHOOSE YOUR OWN ADVENTURE® is a registered trademark of Bantam Books, Inc. Registered in U.S. Patent and Trademark Office and elsewhere.

Concept: Edward Packard; Series Development: R.A. Montgomery and Edward Packard.

Library of Congress Cataloging in Publication Data

Razzi, Jim.
  Pinocchio's adventures.

  (Walt Disney choose your own adventure)
  Summary: The reader shares the adventures of the famous puppet and decides their outcome.
  1. Children's stories, American. 2. Plot-your-own stories. [1. Fairy tales. 2. Puppets—Fiction. 3. Plot-your-own stories] I. Collodi, Carlo, 1826–1890. avventure di Pinocchio. II. Title. III. Series.
PZ8.R22Pi 1985 [E] 84-20461
ISBN: 0-553-05402-3

Published simultaneously in the United States and Canada

Bantam Books are published by Bantam Books, Inc. Its trademark, consisting of the words "Bantam Books" and the portrayal of a rooster, is Registered in U.S. Patent and Trademark Office and in other countries. Marca Registrada. Bantam Books, Inc., 666 Fifth Avenue, New York, New York 10103.

PRINTED IN THE UNITED STATES OF AMERICA

DW 0 9 8 7 6 5 4 3 2 1

READ THIS FIRST!!!

Most books are about other people.

This book is about you—and Pinocchio.

Pinocchio is a little wooden puppet who has magically come alive!

Whatever happens in the story depends on what you decide to do.

Do not read this book from the first page through to the last page. Instead, start at page one and read until you come to your first choice. Decide what you want to do. Then turn to the page shown and see what happens.

When you come to the end of a story, go back and try another choice. Every choice leads to a new adventure—sometimes with a surprising ending! If you're ready to begin, turn to page 1.

Not far from your home, in a small village, lives
Geppetto, a friendly old wood-carver. One day, on
your way to school, you stop by to say hello.

To your surprise, you find Geppetto jumping up
and down with excitement.

"I have made a puppet out of wood!" he shouts.
"And he's alive!"

Geppetto tells you that a few days ago he carved
a wooden puppet and named it Pinocchio.

Turn to page 2.

"Last night, before I went to sleep," Geppetto continues, "I wished upon a star that Pinocchio would be a *real* boy. And the Blue Fairy came and granted my wish!"

"Where is Pinocchio now?" you ask.

"Oh, I have sent him to school." Geppetto laughs. "You see, he is not a real boy just yet. But the Blue Fairy says that when he learns to be brave, truthful, and unselfish, he will be!"

Go on to the next page.

"Say, I'm on my way to school right now!" you cry. "Maybe I can catch up with Pinocchio."

"Yes, yes," says Geppetto. "Hurry up!"

You dash out the door. You can't wait to meet a live puppet!

You hurry down the street. Suddenly you hear a cry coming from a dark alley. Maybe you should see what's wrong. But then you might not catch up with Pinocchio. What should you do?

If you run into the alley, turn to page 4.

If you hurry on your way, turn to page 7.

4   You run into the alley.
    Almost at once, you trip over a small wooden cage. You pick it up. A cricket is inside!
    "Help!" it cries. "Let me out!"
    You can't believe your ears. A talking cricket! Quickly you unlatch the door and let the cricket out.
    "Thanks," it says as it dusts itself off.
    "What—who are you?" you stammer.

Go on to the next page.

"My name is Jiminy Cricket. The Blue Fairy has made me Pinocchio's official conscience. I'm supposed to help him learn right from wrong. But those two rascals, J. Worthington Foulfellow the Fox and Gideon the Cat, trapped me in that cage. And now they are trying to talk Pinocchio into going to Pleasure Island instead of school. I've got to stop them!"

"Let's go!" you cry. "I want to help Pinocchio, too!"

Turn to page 6.

You pop Jiminy in your pocket and dash down the street.

"The coach for Pleasure Island stops somewhere outside the village," shouts Jiminy, "but I don't know where."

Hmm, you think, at one end of the village road is an inn. At the other end is an old farmhouse on the road to the sea. The two places are in opposite directions. Which way should you go?

If you go to the inn, turn to page 16.

If you go the farmhouse, turn to page 13.

You hurry on your way.

Soon you come to the town square. To get to school, you must go around the square by either the right road or the left road.

You try to guess which road Pinocchio might have taken.

If you take the left road, turn to page 8.

If you take the right road, turn to page 10.

You decide to try the left road.

You skip along, hoping to meet Pinocchio.

On your way, you pass the bakery. You love to look in bakery windows!

But if you stop now, you might miss Pinocchio.

If you stop at the bakery, turn to page 22.

If you continue on your way, turn to page 24.

You decide to try the right road.

Halfway down the road, you see a little puppet talking to a fox and a cat.

It must be Pinocchio!

You run up closer.

Now you see that the fox and the cat are two lazy rascals you know very well—J. Worthington Foulfellow and Gideon the Cat!

Go on to the next page.

And at this very moment, they are telling Pinocchio not to go to school! They want him to go to Pleasure Island instead.

You've got to do something!

Maybe you can push the two of them away from Pinocchio. But would that do any good?

It might be better just to talk to Pinocchio.

If you push them away, turn to page 12.

If you talk to Pinocchio, turn to page 27.

12   You barge in and push them away.

"Don't listen to them," you yell. "Pleasure Island is no place for you!"

"Wh-who are you?" stammers Pinocchio.

"A very ill-mannered young person," says J. Worthington.

Pinocchio nods in agreement.

"Wait!" you shout. But it's no use. Pinocchio won't listen. He's off in bad company, and there's nothing you can do now.

The End

You go to the old farmhouse.

No one seems to be around. You peek in a window—and see J. Worthington Foulfellow and Gideon gleefully counting some money!

"Ah, yes," J. Worthington is saying. "I'm glad we told that puppet to go to Pleasure Island. The Coachman paid us well for it. He should be picking Pinocchio up at the Red Lobster Inn right now."

The inn! You chose the wrong place!

Turn to page 14.

14   Suddenly a huge hand scoops Jiminy up.
"Aha! The talking cricket!" booms a big man.
"What a prize for Stromboli's show!"

Stromboli! You've heard of him. He's the cruel
owner of a traveling show.

At that moment, J. Worthington and Gideon run
out of the farmhouse. "That's the cricket I told you
about!" cries J. Worthington.

"Yes," purrs Stromboli. "Here is your reward."

Go on to the next page.

Stromboli glances at you. "You didn't tell Stromboli that the cricket had a friend," he says.

"I didn't know," murmurs J. Worthington. "What shall we do about it?"

"We'll leave him in the farmhouse," he says. "No one goes in there!"

Stromboli ties you up, and the three rascals run off with Jiminy.

You sigh. Poor you—and poor Jiminy. Oh, *why* did you choose the farmhouse?

The End

16   You go to the inn. The coach *is* there. Is
Pinocchio on it? You hop on. *There* he is!
    "Why aren't you in school?" yells Jiminy.
    "Er—it's closed today," Pinocchio answers.
And before your eyes, his nose grows!
    "Remember," says Jiminy, "the Blue Fairy said
a lie will be as plain as the nose on your face."
    "Well, the teacher gave me the day off," says
Pinocchio. And his nose grows even longer!

Turn to page 18.

Jiminy frowns at him. "You see?" he says. "Your nose grew just like your lie."

"I'm sorry I lied!" cries Pinocchio. "The truth is that I want to go to Pleasure Island and have a good time." At that, Pinocchio's nose shrinks back to its normal size.

Now you sit down next to Pinocchio and say hello. "I don't think you should go to Pleasure Island," you add. "I have heard it's a bad place."

Go on to the next page.

"Oh, no," answers Pinocchio. "The Coachman says it's going to be lots of fun!"

You and Jiminy try as hard as you can to make Pinocchio change his mind. But it's no use.

You look at Jiminy and sigh.

"Well," you say, "we had better go along and make sure that nothing bad happens."

"You bet!" says Jiminy.

Turn to page 20.

A little while later, you arrive on Pleasure Island. You can't believe your eyes. It's a big amusement park with children everywhere!

"Hmmp!" sniffs Jiminy. "It seems to me these kids are making jackasses of themselves!"

Pinocchio just laughs and runs off.

Soon you and he are behaving as wildly as everyone else. You can't help yourselves.

Go on to the next page.

The day flies by.

As it is getting dark, you and Pinocchio see a big Fun House. "I'm going in there!" shouts Pinocchio.

"Well, I'm not!" says Jiminy. "That's no place for a cricket. I'll wait outside."

Suddenly you wonder whether *you* should go in. For some strange reason, you're a little frightened of the place.

If you decide to go into the Fun House with Pinocchio, turn to page 26.

If you decide to wait outside with Jiminy, turn to page 30.

You stop to look at the fresh doughnuts in the bakery window. Mmm, do they look good!

The baker sees you and comes out. "Do you like doughnuts?" he asks.

"I sure do!" you answer.

"Then you are in luck. I usually give a treat to the first child who stops by."

He shows you a bagful of little, round doughnut centers. "You can have them," he says.

Go on to the next page.

"Gee, thanks!" you exclaim as you take the bag and hurry on your way.

In a little while, you arrive at the schoolhouse. You have seen no sign of Pinocchio. He must have taken the right road, you think.

Just then, the school bell rings.

Oh, well, you didn't meet Pinocchio, but you do have some delicious doughnut holes for lunch!

The End

You continue on your way.

As you are walking, a classmate of yours runs up. "Look what I found!" he yells.

He shows you a cricket in a wooden cage.

"Let me out!" it cries. "My name is Jiminy Cricket, and I have to find Pinocchio!"

You can't believe your ears. "I'm looking for Pinocchio, too," you exclaim.

"Then set me free!" cries Jiminy.

Go on to the next page.

You ask your friend to free Jiminy and he does.

"Hurry!" cries Jiminy. "I think Pinocchio's taking the coach to Pleasure Island instead of going to school!"

Just then, the coach comes rumbling by!

You and Jiminy try to hop on—but you miss!

Was Pinocchio on the coach? You may never know. But at least you have Jiminy to help you look for him!

The End

26 You decide to go into the Fun House with Pinocchio. Everyone is running wild and doing naughty things! You and Pinocchio join right in.

Suddenly you notice the strangest thing. Everyone has grown a pair of donkey ears and a tail—even you and Pinocchio!

Jiminy was right. You've all been so naughty that you're making jackasses of yourselves!

Turn to page 28.

You run up to Pinocchio. "Excuse me," you say. "You must be Pinocchio. Your father told me all about you."

J. Worthington pushes you roughly aside. "Leave Pinocchio alone. He's coming to Pleasure Island with us."

"Hey!" cries Pinocchio. "What are you doing? I don't think I'll go with you after all."

You sigh with relief. You made the right choice. Now Pinocchio will listen to you.

The End

You and Pinocchio run away and stumble into a large room. It's full of donkeys!

And the Coachman is there yelling, "Come on, you kids! You've had your fun. Now you must pay! I will sell you all for a good price in town!"

"Pinocchio!" you cry. "We have to get out of here!" The two of you run out to tell Jiminy the news.

"Come on!" he yells. "To the sea!"

Go on to the next page.

You run and run.

In the distance, you hear someone shouting. The Coachman must be coming after you!

You come to the edge of a high cliff. You can see the ocean far below.

"Jump, Pinocchio and Jiminy!" you yell. "It's our only chance!"

Pinocchio nods and jumps. You hold your nose and follow with Jiminy. D-O-W-N you go!

Turn to page 32.

30   You decide to wait with Jiminy.

You both go to the back of the Fun House.

You wait and wait, but no one comes out.

Finally a big door opens, and a bunch of donkeys come out! They're all wearing children's clothes!

What's going on? you wonder.

Then you see the Coachman. He's cracking his whip and herding the donkeys into crates.

Go on to the next page.

"Come on, you kids!" the Coachman shouts. "You've had your fun. Now you must work!"

"Oh, no!" gasps Jiminy. "Those children made jackasses of themselves for *real*!"

Suddenly you see a little donkey with Pinocchio's clothes on.

"Pinocchio! Is that you?" you ask.

The sad little donkey opens its mouth to speak, but all it can say is "Hee-haw, hee-haw!"

The End

You hit the water with a splash and find a piece of driftwood to hang on to.

You and Pinocchio start paddling. But which way should you go? All you can see is Pleasure Island.

Go on to the next page.

Finally you spot something large and smooth rising out of the water. If you climb on top, you might see better. But what is the thing? It looks like a rock, but . . . maybe you should forget the idea and just paddle away.

If you decide to paddle toward the rock, turn to page 34.

If you decide to paddle away from the rock, turn to page 36.

34   You decide to paddle toward the rock.
      Suddenly it moves. It's not a rock—it's Monstro
the Whale!
      You and Pinocchio paddle wildly to get out of
Monstro's path. You are almost out of danger when
you hear a cry. It's Jiminy!

Go on to the next page.

Jiminy has slipped off the driftwood and is floating helplessly in the water, right in front of Monstro!

You want to try to save the little cricket, but you're afraid. You might be swallowed by Monstro.

Then Jiminy shouts, "Don't worry about me. Save yourself and Pinocchio. I'll be okay!"

You don't know what to do.

If you swim back to get Jiminy, turn to page 40.

If you listen to Jiminy, turn to page 39.

You paddle away from the rock.

You have traveled a short distance when you hear a loud gurgling sound. A huge, round head rises out of the water.

It's a giant octopus! The huge creature grabs you with one of its slimy legs.

"Yeow!" you yell.

You struggle to get free, but the octopus drags you under. It looks like the end for you. . . .

Go on to the next page.

Suddenly you hear: "Stop that, Octavio!"

You look around in surprise and see a tiny mermaid. "Let go!" she shouts at the octopus.

Slowly the huge creature releases you. He slides back in the water with a gurgle.

The little mermaid smiles.

"Octavio is just a big baby," she says. "He didn't mean any harm. I hope none of you was frightened."

Turn to page 38.

"Well, *I* was!" shouts Jiminy. "You should watch your pets more carefully, young lady!"

"I'm sorry," says the mermaid. "And to make up for it, I will lead you all to safety."

Soon you are standing on a beach close to home, waving good-bye to the mermaid.

You're safe. Only one thing bothers you. How are you going to explain your donkey ears and tail to your parents?

The End

You decide to listen to Jiminy.

But when you turn around to see how he's doing, Monstro swallows him up!

You should have gone back for him!

Suddenly the Blue Fairy appears. "You made the wrong choice," she says, "but I will save your friend."

You and Pinocchio smile at each other. You are very lucky to know a fairy who can fix your mistakes!

The End

40　　　You swim back to get Jiminy.

"Wait!" yells Pinocchio. "I'll help, too."

You and Pinocchio reach Jiminy, but Monstro is right there, and he swallows you up!

You are swimming around in his stomach when you see a boat with a man in it. It's Geppetto!

You all yell and swim toward the boat.

"Oh, Pinocchio!" cries Geppetto. "I'm so glad I found you!"

Go on to the next page.

Geppetto tells you he heard that Pinocchio had gone to Pleasure Island. "I came to look for him, but on the way, Monstro swallowed me!"

Pinocchio bows his head. "I know I did wrong, Father," he says. "I'm sorry now."

You look around. "How will we get out of here?" you ask sadly.

"I don't know," answers Geppetto. "But I'll build a fire for now. You must all be cold."

Turn to page 42.

Geppetto builds a huge, smoky fire . . . and the smoke makes Monstro sneeze. "AHH-CHOO!"

You all fly out of Monstro's mouth, into the water. You're free! And you're near the shore.

But Monstro is mad and charges at you.

"Quick!" yells Pinocchio. "Head for the shore. I'll let Monstro come after me!"

"No!" you yell. Then you watch in horror as the brave puppet disappears beneath a wave.

Go on to the next page.

A few minutes later, you reach the shore.
Pinocchio is there, too. He was washed up beside
you but is lying very still. "My poor boy," cries
Geppetto. "You gave your life to save us."

Out of nowhere, the Blue Fairy appears. She
smiles at Pinocchio. "You have been brave, truthful,
and unselfish," she says. "Arise, Pinocchio!"

Pinocchio stands up. He's a *real* boy!

You sigh. Everything is all right again. Even your
ears and tail are gone. Best of all, now Pinocchio can
be a *real* friend!

The End